S0-CFX-171

THE BOOK THAT NO ONE WANTED TO READ

THE BOOK THAT NO ONE WANTED TO READ

RICHARD AYOADE

ILLUSTRATED BY
TOR FREEMAN

WALKER BOOKS

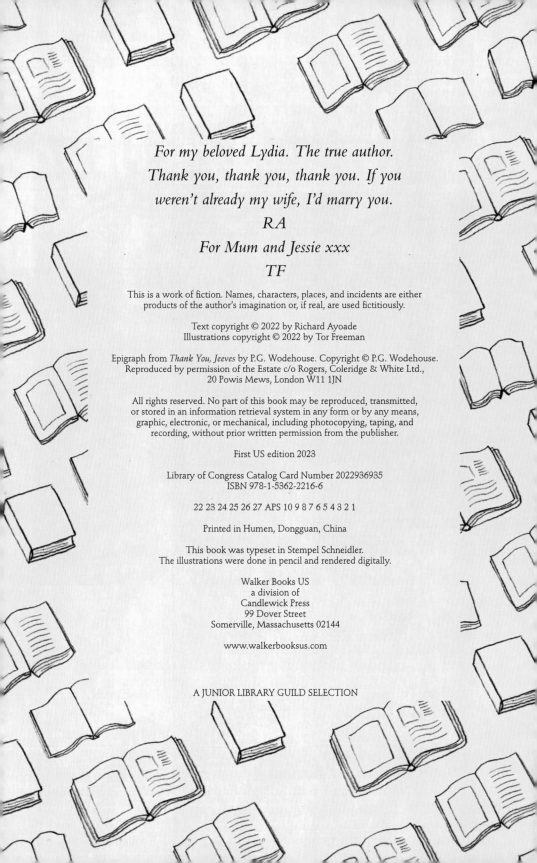

For my beloved Lydia. The true author.
Thank you, thank you, thank you. If you
weren't already my wife, I'd marry you.
RA
For Mum and Jessie xxx
TF

Text copyright © 2022 by Richard Ayoade
Illustrations copyright © 2022 by Tor Freeman

Epigraph from *Thank You, Jeeves* by P.G. Wodehouse. Copyright © P.G. Wodehouse. Reproduced by permission of the Estate c/o Rogers, Coleridge & White Ltd., 20 Powis Mews, London W11 1JN

First US edition 2023

Library of Congress Catalog Card Number 2022936935
ISBN 978-1-5362-2216-6

22 23 24 25 26 27 APS 10 9 8 7 6 5 4 3 2 1

Printed in Humen, Dongguan, China

This book was typeset in Stempel Schneidler.
The illustrations were done in pencil and rendered digitally.

Walker Books US
a division of
Candlewick Press
99 Dover Street
Somerville, Massachusetts 02144

www.walkerbooksus.com

A JUNIOR LIBRARY GUILD SELECTION

"Well, here I am, what?"

~ Bertie Wooster in *Thank You, Jeeves,*
by P.G. Wodehouse

INTRODUCTION

IN WHICH I (A BOOK) ASK SEVERAL
IMPORTANT QUESTIONS, SUCCESSFULLY
ANSWER THEM, AND GENERALLY GET
THINGS OFF TO A SUPERB START

What is it that makes you want to read a book?

They say you should never judge a book by its cover. But how else can you decide whether you might like it?

You can't read a book to figure out whether you want to read that book because, by that stage, you will have already read it.

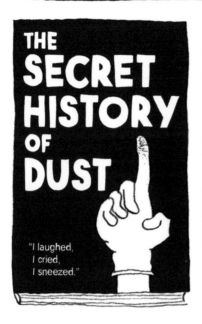

Fig. 1

BOOK COVERS
(VARIOUS)

That's why us books always try to make our covers look fun. But we know (from bitter experience) that even if we adorn ourselves with a majestic sparkly unicorn or a magical fearsome dragon, the battle is far from won. How can we forget the times we've been hurled across the room, left under whiffy pant piles, or, worse, shelved, forever collecting dust? *What's so bad about being on a dusty shelf?* you might say. But you've never been a book. I have a very bad dust allergy and no nose. Where are those sneezes going?

Oh yes.
I'm a book.
Hello.

I suppose you might think it's weird that a book is saying "Hello." Well, why *shouldn't* a book say hello? We're not animals. Although (oddly) you seem very happy to read about animals saying hello and doing all sorts of other things that don't seem too realistic, like tigers sitting at tables eating iced buns and not biting your head off.

Here's a tip. If you see a tiger in your house, get out of your house.

If you want to make friends with an animal, at least pick one that doesn't eat people.*

Fig. 2: THE CAPYBARA (*Hydrochoerus hydrochaeris*)
THE LARGEST RODENT IN THE WORLD (NOT TO SCALE)
(SCARF: MODEL'S OWN)

* Might I suggest getting on good terms with the capybara? This is just about the friendliest mammal you could meet. Native to Central and South America, they eat grass, weigh up to 150 pounds, and look like someone pushed a kangaroo's head through a squirrel's tail. They have dry skin and swim to a high standard. By the way, what you just read is called a footnote. It's not something you scribble on your toes; it's a note at the bottom or "foot" of the page.

1. Spot tiger

2. Exit house

Fig. 3

HOW TO SPOT A TIGER
IS IN YOUR HOUSE

Sorry. I do get angry occasionally. Do you? Here are The Top Five Things That Grate My Gears.

1. *People who fold the corner of the page to save their place.* Have these savages not heard of novelty bookmarks? Or paper? Or "memory"? Which part of *your* body would you most like to have folded back on itself?

2. *People who underline certain words.* ALL THE WORDS ARE IMPORTANT!

3. *People who skip to the end.* If the end was meant to come sooner, it'd be called "the middle."

4. *People who give up after one paragraph.* What are you afraid of? Wasting another twelve seconds?

6. *My difficulty with counting.* Now, as you may have guessed from the title, I'm going to tell you a story about a Book That No One Wanted To Read. It's a very moving story,

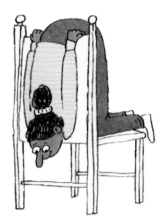

Assisted Fold

Simple Back Fold

Curled Arm Fold
(aka the whirlpool)

Roll Fold

Rainbow Fold

Zigzag Fold

Very, Very Slight Fold

Fig. 4

BODY FOLDING
(VARIOUS EXAMPLES)

and I can say with all modesty that this might be the most important book of all time. Why? Because it's the first book to have been *written by a book*. Most books are written by *authors*. Take it from me, authors can be quite annoying. They go on and on, filling up page after page, but they have no idea what it's like to *be* a book. They think we exist just to please them! What do *they* know about the *real* experience of being a book?

Well, that's about to change.

I'm in charge now, so stand back* and fasten your seat belts—it's going to be a bumpy read.

---

*But don't stand back too far otherwise you won't be able to read the book. Unless you're looking through binoculars, in which case may I ask, "Why are you looking through binoculars?" And, furthermore, why are you standing up with your seat belt on? Sit down! I'm trying to write this thing!

Fig. 5

SUGGESTED DISTANCE
BETWEEN YOU AND THIS BOOK

1. Too close

2. Too far

3. Just right

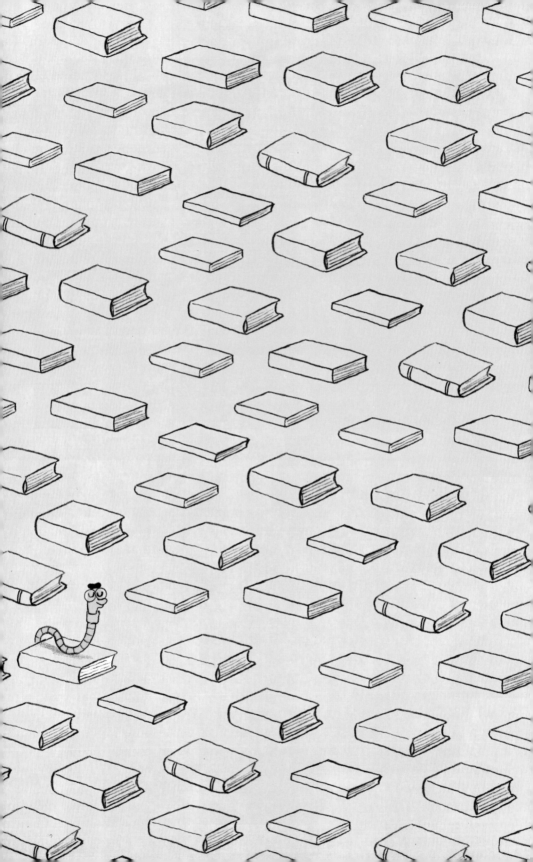

CHAPTER ONE

IN WHICH I TELL THE IMMORTAL (AND BEST-SELLING*) STORY OF THE BOOK THAT NO ONE WANTED TO READ

The Book That No One Wanted To Read did not have a cover design that was sparkly or magical or scary. The Book That No One Wanted To Read didn't have a cover design at all. Unless you call "plain" a design. The only memorable thing about it was . . . no: it's gone.

---

*Depending on how it sells. By the way, I never understand why books that sell a lot of copies are called *best-sellers*. What was *best* about how they were sold? They just sold "more" than other books. They *should* be called *more-sellers*.

The only impression The Book That No One Wanted To Read made was of making no impression whatsoever. It was a murky kind of non-color, like something dully reflected in a bog. Or, say you stared at a school lunch table for a little while and let your eyes drift so that, after about an hour, everything was just a blur, a flat sort of nothing that you couldn't describe. That's what this book looked like. Or, to put it as an equation: Level of Fun on Cover of Book = Nil.

And as for what was inside . . .

Imagine the driest leaf you ever saw. One of those leaves that, were you to pick it up, would crumble like a stepped-on cracker.

A leaf that, if it were subject to the barest of breezes, would break into a billion solemn specks.

Well, compared to this book, such a leaf is like

LAUGHTER
+
KINDNESS
−
SELF-PITY
=
FUN

Fun as an equation

OCCASIONAL PERIL

NAUGHTINESS (MODERATE)

LAUGHTER

PLAY

HIGH JINKS (VARIOUS)

SILLINESS

LARKS

Fun as a pie chart

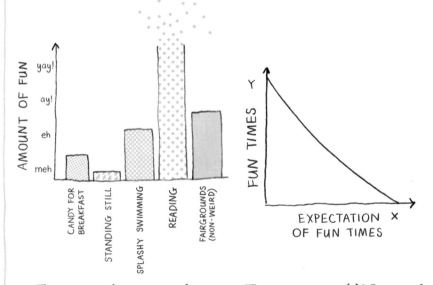

Fun as a bar graph

Fun as an XY graph

Fig. 6

FUN

a lush tropical garden besprinkled by the soft spray of a waterfall.

The Book That No One Wanted To Read was so deathly dry that even bookworms gave it the swerve. "We can't digest it," they'd say. "It's like sucking on cement." So off they'd go to more accommodating books in which they could both bed and breakfast.

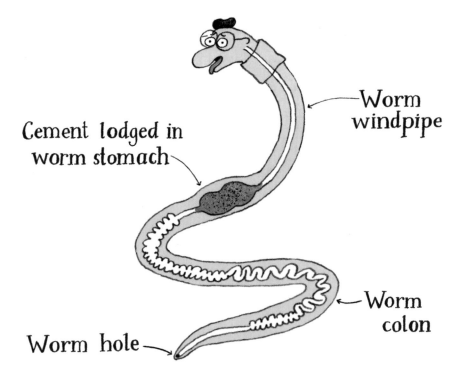

Fig. 7: BOOKWORM DIGESTIVE TRACT
(POST-CEMENT-SUCK)

There are people who say they like the way books smell. Well, these people had never smelled The Book That No One Wanted To Read. The Book That No One Wanted To Read was a musty old stinker, mingling the aroma of mold, the dankness of dust-smothered moss, and the far-off scent of gym socks. But we cannot blame The Book That No One Wanted To Read for its offensive odor; it's not like it could wash.

Books don't do too well in the shower. Nor the bath. Even a damp cloth can prove too much for us. We go all sad and see-through. And when we dry out (*if* we dry out) we start to expand. Before long we're a puffy disgrace that can barely stand up straight. Some of us literally fall apart. Others become (gasp) *illegible.*

To us books, the word *illegible* is one of the scariest words in that top book (and close personal friend) the dictionary. Do you know what it means? *Illegible* means that something is impossible, or nearly impossible, to read because it is so unclear.

If a book becomes illegible, what is it?

Have you heard the old philosophical question: "If a tree falls in a forest, and no one is there to hear it, does it make a sound?"

Well, I know the answer to that philosophical question. The answer is:

Yes.
It does.
Obvs.

I also know the sound it makes. And that sound is *Ow!!*

You see, I know, because us books are *there*. Paper *comes from trees*. This means we were once *inside* those trees. And when no one else is around (trust me), those lads let rip.*

---

*Or to put it another way, trees aren't always the strong and silent type. After a fall they don't hold back with the language. You know, the kinds of things your parents shout and then quickly say, "Don't repeat that in school."

Fig. 8

THE SILENCE OF
THE FOREST

The idea behind the "If a tree falls in the forest" problem is really about sound. *What is a sound?* A sound must be *heard.* And if no one is there to hear it, can a sound exist?

I sometimes wonder whether the same is true of us books. If no one can read us, what *are* we?

If no one *sees* you, are you even a person? How would you know you were real? You'd be invisible!*

Us books need to be seen. We need to be held. We need to be heard. I think that's why children make the best readers, because they know that these things are also true of them.**

By now you're probably thinking, all this is fine if you enjoy a book moaning for fifty hours, but

---

*Problems with invisibility include people bumping into you, and not coming out well in photos.

**I don't know if that's true. I'm just trying to get you on my side.

Fig. 9

INVISIBILITY
(PROBLEMS WITH)

what about the *story*? When are you going to get on with it and say some more about The Book That No One Wanted To Read? Because, at the moment (or maybe a little before this moment if you're being truly honest), you're thinking that *this* is The Book That No One Wanted To Read. To which I'd say, control your camel—the story *is* coming. And (anyway) we are a *little way* into our adventure.

We now know how The Book That No One Wanted To Read looked (sort of blah), felt (v dry), and smelled (not good), but what of its contents?

For a book isn't a mere object. It's like a delivery vehicle: a packed truck that pulls up outside your head, laden with language and story and ideas.

That's why when you say to your friend, "Did you read so and so?" you know that they *don't* have to read *your* copy of the book in

Camel Fence

Camel Wrangling

Camel Semaphore

Camel Shaming

Fig. 10

CAMEL CONTROL

(VARIOUS METHODS)

order to give you an answer. What you're really asking is, "Did that packed truck laden with language and story and ideas pull up alongside your head as well?" In other words, did you like what the book was about? And in *other* other words, did you like the way it was told?

Fig. 11: IDEAS TRUCK
(DELIVERY METHOD)

It's a book's *insides* that set it apart. A book fashioned from solid gold, encrusted with jewels, gossamer pages ruffled by the sweet breath of angels, can still be a *bore*.

What (exactly) were the *contents* of The Book That No One Wanted To Read?

It's a trick question.

No one knew.

Because no one had ever opened The Book That No One Wanted To Read, on account of no one wanting to read it. Ever.

But (one day) that all changed . . .

CHAPTER TWO

IN WHICH I (YOUR FAVORITE BOOK AND FOREVER FRIEND) SET THE SCENE, INTRODUCE YOU TO YOU, AND VERY MUCH GET ON WITH IT

Let's say a little more about this "one day" because (if you think about it) all days are "one day." What made this day *particular*?

Well, what made this day particular was that on *this* particular day a particular child walked into a particular library that housed a particular Book That No One Wanted To Read. Would you mind imagining that particular library for me?

I'm new to storytelling and I'm keen to set the right mood.

IS IT BIG OR SMALL?

I agree. Big seems more appropriate.

NEW OR OLD?

Yes. Old seems right. It feels like The Book That No One Wanted To Read has been in this library for quite some time.

SHALL WE MAKE THE LIBRARY A LITTLE COBWEBBY?

I know what you mean—that might make this whole story feel a bit too spooky. This is a library, not a haunted house. But let's make it a little fusty-smelling. Nothing unpleasant— it's just that this place isn't exactly on friendly terms with a feather duster.

Now, shall we turn our attention to the child?

Yes . . . let's meet this *particular* child. But we have to be careful not to make this child *too* particular.

Fig. 12: THIS CHILD
(NON-PARTICULAR)

For example, if I said this particular child was an eight-year-old girl with red pigtails who lived in Ipswich and was able to breathe fire, you might think, "That's nothing like me. My hair is brown and curly. Also, why would anyone live in Ipswich?"*

Fig. 13: GIRL
(FIRE-BREATHING)

---

*I used to live in Ipswich, so I can be rude about it, just like you can be rude about your brother/sister/friend/parent. But if anyone *else* is rude about them, watch out. But try not to be *too* rude to your brother/sister/friend/parent. They are your brother/sister/friend/parent after all.

Each one of us is particular, but very often the people in books don't seem very particular at all. They're just strong or handsome or beautiful or charming—or else they're a villain. I think we should try something different.

Handsome Prince   Wicked Witch   Comedy Sidekick

Fig. 14: STOCK CHARACTERS
(THREE EXAMPLES)

How would *you* describe yourself? There's no need to look in a mirror. A mirror won't show anything more than the light bouncing off your face. That's your cover, in a manner of speaking. And by now, we know something about The Trouble With Covers. What's underneath? What are you actually *like*?

Fig. 15: THIS MIRROR WILL NOT HELP YOU SEE YOURSELF

Because that's what this *particular* child—this character—is like.

YOU.

In fact, we're even going to call this character "you."

Also, let's not tell this story as if it's something that's happened, because I don't know what's happened. This story is happening *now*. It's *unfolding*. Or (to be less fancy about it), I'm making it up as I go along.

So, in summary:

Time = now

Place = library

Main character = you

CHAPTER THREE

AND (HAVING ESTABLISHED THAT I'M A BOOK AND YOU ARE YOU) OFF WE SORT-OF GO

You are ambling along the endless aisles of an enormous library when you realize that you have lost your way.

You creep cautiously along looming walls lined with **LITERATURE** and **POETRY**, **ART** and **ARCHITECTURE**.

☛ This way **BIOGRAPHIES**.

☞ That way **BIBLIOGRAPHIES**.

You slink past **CERAMICS**, **COMPUTER SCIENCE**, **DRAMA**, and **DATA MANAGEMENT**;

down to **DICTIONARIES** and on to **ENCYCLOPEDIAS**; right by racks of **MAGAZINES**, **MANUSCRIPTS**, and **PERIODICALS** in every language;

brushing by **BOOKS OF ANTIQUITY**; past piles of **PHILOSOPHY**, **PSYCHOLOGY**, and **HISTORY**;

studies of **SPACE** and **COSMOLOGY**; tomes of **THEOLOGY** and edicts on **ETHICS**; soundless swathes of **SCIENCE** and **SOCIOLOGY**;

miles of **MATHEMATICS**, **PNEUMATICS**, and **MECHANICS**;

packed stacks of **ELECTRICITY**, **ECONOMICS**, and **ASTRONOMY**; and even writing about **WRITING**: how to write, what to write, and why we write in the first place; all next to twenty-five aisles of books about how to **GET RICH**.

You wonder whether you'll ever be able to get back out, when you wander into a mysterious nook marked **MISCELLANY**.

MISCELLANY sounds like a path you might take by mistake, like WHOOPSYROADY. Which seems appropriate. You are, after all, quite uncertain as to where you are.

You feel like you're somewhere *forgotten*. Or (and maybe this is nearer the mark) in a place that you could *only* discover by taking a wrong turn.

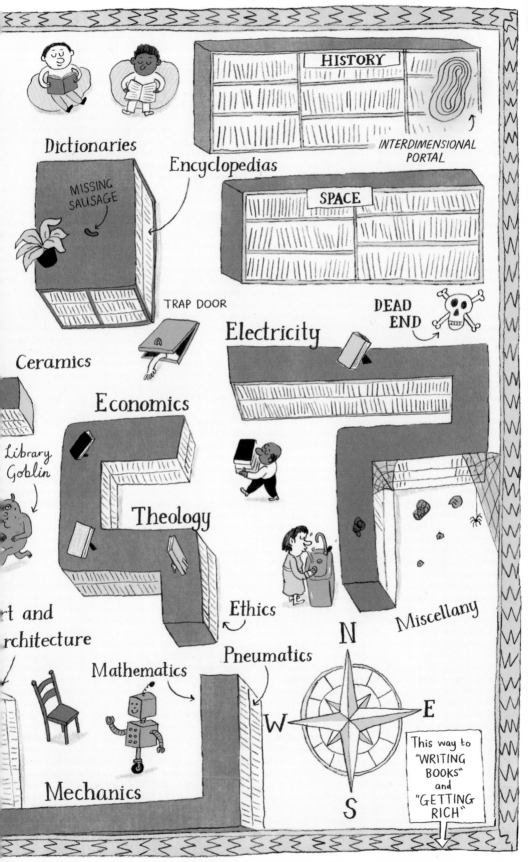

What, you ask yourself, is meant by *miscellany*? Fortunately, this is a library, so you leaf through one of its dictionaries. A brief thumb tells you that *miscellany* is a noun and can mean either:

1. a collection of writings on various subjects or

2. a mixture of various items.

Whoever organized this section must have had the second in mind, because the only thing uniting the books in Miscellany is that they don't seem to belong anywhere else. Not that there are many books here. Even though the aisle stretches away as far as you can see, it can't contain more than a dozen or so books, each one looking misplaced and lonely. And as you consider the kinds of books that would end up in this avenue of the uncategorizable, your eyes fall upon one in particular.*

---

*When people say their "eyes fall on" something, I always imagine their eyes dropping out of their head and landing with a squelch. Now you can, too!

Fig. 17: EYES FALLING

On a high-up shelf, on its own, leaning against a rusting bookend, is a slim, unmarked volume. Its cover seems like it's made from worn-through corduroy, its color hovering between the indistinct green of lichen and the dirty gray of a paving slab. You find yourself staring at it for longer than you would have thought you might stare at an unremarkable book.

After a while you start to get a funny feeling. *This book doesn't want me to look at it,* you think. *This book is actually trying to get me to look away.*

And being a curious sort of child (the kind who would leave no box unopened), you know what you must do.

So you search for something to stand on.

And now you're carrying a small library ladder toward the book.

And now you're halfway up that ladder.

And that's when you hear a low voice.

A voice that sounds like dust.

Stilts

Another Person
(ask permission first)

Robust Fruit

Fig. 18

THINGS TO STAND ON
(VARIOUS)

CHAPTER FOUR

IN WHICH YOU FIND YOURSELF HAVING A (RATHER LONG) TALK WITH A BOOK

This low voice, the dusty one, says one word. And that word is

– Hey!

Less brave children than you might be startled at hearing such a voice. But you are not one of those less brave children. You are steadfast. You are from Ipswich.* So you say,

---

*If you're not from Ipswich, please ignore this last sentence about being from Ipswich. And also, congratulations!

- Hello?

in a voice that, if it *is* a little wobbly, remains as strong as a lion's roar. And when no one answers, you know exactly what to say next.

- Who said that?

And you are only trembling a tiny teensy amount when you hear that cracked voice again.

– I'd advise you to look at the other books. They're far more interesting than me.

- Who are you?

you say, with more of the straightforward bravery for which you are known.

– I am a book

is the reply.

Fig. 19: A SLIGHT TREMBLE

Scared though you are, you can't help laughing a little at this. Emboldened, you decide to sort out this nonsense sooner rather than later.

- Very funny. Where are you hiding?

– I told you. I am a book.

Fig. 20

GETTING A BOOK TO
ADMIT IT'S A BOOK
(DIFFICULTY WITH)

Getting someone to admit that they're not a book is less easy than you'd hoped. Who can blame you when your (normally remarkable) patience starts to wear thin? It's no surprise (therefore) when you say,

- Stop being weird. It's getting freaky.

– I am not being weird. Nor do I get "freaky." I am a book. I do not wish to have to say it a fourth time. I do not wish to be plucked from my resting place. I find it rather upsetting to be picked up, flicked through, and slammed shut. It actually gives me this shooting pain right through my spine.

- If no one picks you up, how do you expect anyone to read you?

– I don't expect anyone to read me, nor has anyone *ever* *wanted* to read me, and I plan on keeping it that way.

– That's ridiculous.

– You're the one talking to a book.

And this is the point when you wonder whether you and your mind are on the same team. You *are* a tad tired. You are (despite your unquestionably heroic nature) a *little* jittery. Your imagination (it almost goes without saying) is immense. Perhaps this is some kind of waking dream?

The voice continues.

Fig. 21: BODY AND MIND TRACK-AND-FIELD EVENT
(RELAY RACE), WINNER UNKNOWN

– You're probably wondering how a book can speak, seeing as books don't have mouths.

– How did you know that?

– It's because I am telepathic. Do you know what that means?

– Yes. But it's hard to describe.

– If you can't describe it, you don't know what it means.

– I know what the word *pompous* means.

– How fascinating. Do you want to know what *telepathic* means?

And though it pains you to say yes, you say,

– Yes.

– *Telepathic* means you can send your thoughts to someone else's mind, and then receive their thoughts back. You are aware, I take it, that you are in a library?

You are (indeed) aware of this. You practically invented this library just a little while ago, but you don't want to humiliate the poor thing, so you confine yourself to a dignified

– Uh-huh.

– Have you noticed any shushing?

– Any shushing?

– Has anyone shushed you?

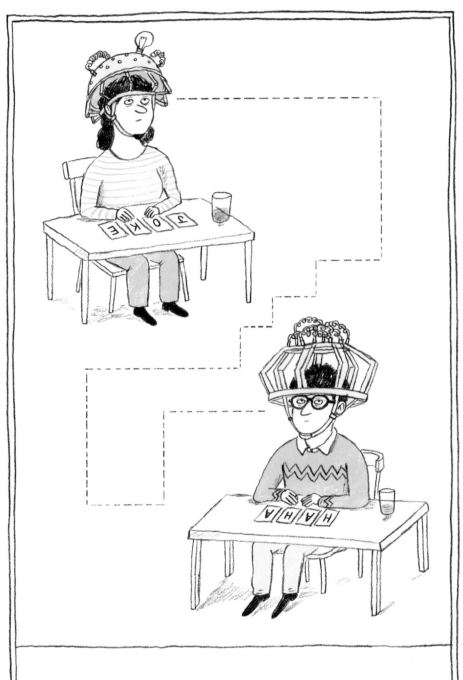

Fig. 22

TELEPATHY

You pause to ponder. You have (thus far) been un-shushed. You say so.

– Do you not find it strange that you have not been shushed, given that we have been talking for the past however long?

– I'm not sure that's the strangest thing that's happening.

– But I did not ask you whether not being shushed was more strange than other things. I merely asked whether it was strange. You see, the librarian here is a well-known shusher. I saw someone drop a handkerchief on the floor, and the librarian gave them a fearful shushing. Do you know how much noise a dropped handkerchief makes?

You do not bother to say, *Not a lot of noise.*

– You're right. Not a lot of noise,

says the voice.

Handkerchief
(almost silent)

Ornamental Bowl
(quiet)

Drum Kit
(loud)

Angry Hen
(ear-shattering)

Fig. 23

LOUDNESS OF DIFFERENT DROPPED ITEMS

(IN ASCENDING ORDER OF LOUDNESS)

It continues:

– The reason you have not been shushed is because we've been speaking telepathically. You have not been shushed because you have not made a single shushable sound.

You open your mouth slightly. Your throat (you realize) has been still. You haven't opened it since you first heard that strange voice. You lift up a hand to check that your neck is still there. It is. You do not say

– How?

out loud, yet still the voice replies.

– I have no idea how. It's never worked before. This is my first telepathic exchange.

The idea that this book can read your thoughts is not entirely welcome to you. Many of the things that gallop through your gray matter aren't quite fit for broadcast. Certain notions

Fig. 24: THOUGHTS (UNFIT FOR BROADCAST)

that skip through your noggin are best kept there. You will have to keep a tight (non-actual) grip on your brain.

This is super weird, you don't say.

– Yes. Rather.

– Well. Bye, I guess.

– Bye.

CHAPTER FIVE

IN WHICH YOU (AND THE STORY) TAKE A TURN

You tell yourself (mid-walk-away) that what happened cannot have happened. There is simply no such thing as telepathy and (if there were) how would a *book* be capable of it? You're going to go home, lie down, sleep, wake up, and hope no further procedures are necessary.

You make your way through the stacks, past Horror and Humor, Conspiracy and Clay, but before you even reach Anger Management, you bump into a beetling browser in the Biography section. And, being one of the Top Ten Polite People Of All Time In Any Given Bump-Into Situation, you say, in your lowest library voice,

- Sorry.

And within (say) one quarter of a millisecond, you hear a sharp "Shush!"

You look over. The librarian's crooked finger bisects her pursed lips. The propulsive force of her sibilance flecks her digit with spittle.

It's kind of gross. But you cannot fault her hearing.

- Hmmm.

- Yes, hmmm,

says a voice. A voice that is not nearby. A voice that no one else can hear. A voice that sounds

View A:
Full frontal

View B:
Cubist

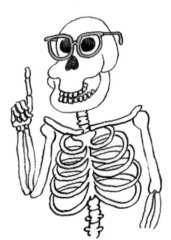

View C:
Skeletal

View D:
Extreme close-up

Fig. 25

LIBRARIAN FINGER,
SPITTLE-FLECKED

(VARIOUS VIEWS)

like That Book That Obviously Can't Have A
Voice On Account Of It Being A Book.

You now have a choice. You could do what
many would do: run, do some light screaming,
and take your shushing like a trooper . . .

Freezing

Running

Skipping

Hiding

Fig. 26: RESPONSE OPTIONS WHEN TERRIFIED
(A SELECTION)

But you are not many others. I mean, how many chances do you get to have a telepathic conversation with a book in a library powered purely by your own imagination? Fewer than you'd think. So back you march.

– Why don't you want anyone to read you?

– None of your business.

– Is that why you're so high up? So that no one can get to you?

– Do you think I put *myself* up here?

– I don't know—I suppose I figured a book that can speak could probably float or something.

– Don't be absurd.

– You think *I'm* absurd? I think you're absurd! What does *absurd* mean?

– Absurd means *silly*.

– Yes. You are definitely that.

– No one forced you to come back here. You are free to go. Unlike me, who has to stay where I'm put.

You feel bad now. Books can be so manipulative.

Fig. 27
CONVERSATION STARTERS

– Would you like me to take you down?

– No I would not.

Sometimes (if the conversation isn't quite flowing) it can help to change the subject.

Fig. 28

CONVERSATION STOPPERS

– So, what kind of book are you?

– The kind of book that is perfectly happy to remain out of reach.

– Do you bite?

– What?

– Do you have teeth? Can you bite?

– Of course not! I am a book!

– Who happens to be able to talk.

– Only telepathically. We've already established that I don't have a mouth, so how could I have teeth?

The book realizes that it's said too much.

– Hey! Don't get any ideas. Stay where you are.

– Or what? You'll bite me, will you?

You move toward the ladder.

Fig. 29

THINGS THAT HAVE TEETH

Dog's Skull

This Alligator

Comb

Windup
Teeth Toy

Handsaw

Fig. 30

THINGS THAT DO NOT
HAVE TEETH

Some
Lumps

This Tiny
Baby

Frog
Puppet

The Book
That No One
Wanted To Read

Most Socks

– Ooh! You rotten louse. That was a mean trick. Leave me alone. What have I ever done to you?

– Take over my head without asking?

– Other than that?

Fig. 31: COMMON LOUSE

Fig. 32: ROTTEN LOUSE

– Any final words before I take you down?

– Buzz off.

But you've already started climbing up.

– I don't want to disappoint anyone,

it says.

You stop halfway up the ladder, as if to say "Oh." Which wasn't the plan, but the problem with having plans is that things don't always go to them. Plans tend to change. Which is more or less the same as there being no plan at all.

Perhaps a short interlude might do us some good right now?

I think we deserve one. After all, this is quite a lot to take in . . .

MUSICAL INTERLUDE

—

THE RECORDS
THAT NO ONE
WANTED TO HEAR

TONY TAPEWORM
AND THE PARASITES

GOTTA
SCRAT
THAT
ITCH

THE ELEPHANT

TRUNK FOOD

The Sheep

ROCK AROUND THE FLOCK

LARRY LORRY AND
THE TRUCKSTOP ANGELS

DOUBLE-PARKED

The Muff
FLOUR POW

CHAPTER SIX

IN WHICH THE BOOK (IN A MANNER OF SPEAKING) OPENS UP

You're halfway up the ladder (neither here nor there) with no plan to speak of and a funny feeling in your middle.

– What do you mean you don't want to disappoint anyone?

The book doesn't answer right away. It makes a slight shuffling sound, as if it tried to turn one of its pages but thought better of it.

– I'm worried that if anyone *did* take me down from up here, they'd be disappointed.

– Well, if no one takes you down, how will you know *what* people think of you?

– Exactly.

– But that's bad.

– That's one way of looking at it. Another way of looking at it is: what you don't know won't bother you.

– What do you have to lose?

– Everything.

– Don't be so dramatic.

– I'm supposed to be dramatic. I'm a book. If there's no drama, there's no story!

And it's at this point that we might wonder whether this *is* a story.

1. INTRODUCTION OF THE ACTION

2. RISING ACTION OR CONFLICT

3. CLIMAX OR HIGH POINT OF THE CONFLICT

4. FALLING ACTION OR COMPROMISE

5. RESOLUTION OR CONCLUSION

Fig. 33

DRAMA

(AN EXAMPLE OF)

It's really just two people (actually, make that one person) silently talking to some paper.*

   - I'm always reading books at school that have no drama and no story,

you say.

   – No one *wants* to read them, though. People just *have* to read them.

   - Belinda Lee Todd wants to read them. She loves school. She does math in her spare time.

   – What does she look like?

   - Neat. Shiny teeth.

   – Those are bad signs.

   - That's what I thought. And her initials spell out my least favorite sandwich.

---

*Which sounds a little like writing . . .

GOALS

4:30 AM WAKE UP ♡
4:31 AM Start interval ♡
training workout
4:47 AM Meditate
5:11 AM math
5:23 AM BREAKFAST: Bone broth,
spinach, hard-boiled egg

5:40 AM Extra math
5:48 AM More math
5:51 AM Extra more math
5:59 AM Online philosophy
seminar (teaching)
6:18 AM SIT-UPS
6:20 AM Water break
6:21 AM End of water break
6:22 AM one-armed push-ups
6:25 AM Wake up Parents

#BUSY!
Be Fearless! cont. overleaf! ♡
☆YOU CAN DO IT!☆

Fig. 34

BELINDA LEE TODD'S
DAY PLANNER
(EXTRACT)

1. The shuffle into position

2. The big leap

3. The moment of contact

4. The time for regret

Fig. 35

BOOK ATTACK
(PROPOSED)

– If she comes in here I'll drop onto her head.

– Oh, she wouldn't come in here. She doesn't read for fun. She only reads textbooks.

– Another bad sign.

It feels quite nice to talk to someone about old BLT. You wouldn't want to complain about her to another person, because that other person might not understand that it's wrong to enjoy math. But there's no real *harm* in telling your problems to a book.* I mean, who else is it going to tell?

– Exactly,

says the book. Which is when you start to think, well, if you're going to keep talking (albeit telepathically) to a book, it feels a bit odd to call the book "Book."

---

*Which also sounds a little like writing . . .

– So what should I call you?

– I don't know.

– What do you mean you don't know?

– I don't know what I'm called.

– Well, what's your title?

– I don't have a title.

– You must have a title. All books have a title. Otherwise you wouldn't know what they're about.

– Well, I don't know what I'm about.

– What's written on your spine?

– What's written on yours?

– Why would there be anything written on my spine?

– Why would there be anything written on mine?

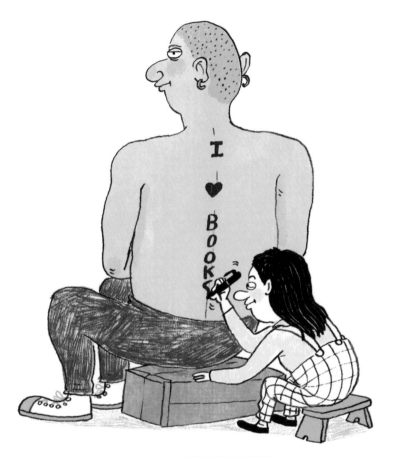

Fig. 36: SPINE-WRITING

- Because you're a book!

- That's bookist!

- That's not a thing!

– Oh, so *you* get to decide what is and what isn't bookist? Typical non-book behavior.

– What are you talking about?

– How people treat books. They have no respect. They act like they own them.

– Isn't that because people *do* own them?

– I don't know how you sleep. Books aren't just property. They're not just things. They're alive!

– But aren't they also things?

– So are you.

You're not sure about this. The book's not done, though. In fact, it's pretty far from done. Let's just say, if "done" were a place, we'd be flying long-haul.

Pampering

Massage

Adoration

Fig. 37

HOW TO TREAT A BOOK WELL
(THREE SUGGESTIONS)

– Do you know what happens to books that no one wants to read?

– I don't know. People give them to thrift shops?

– That's not quite true.

– How come?

– Because those books are wanted.

Fig. 38
ITEMS
FOUND
IN
THRIFT
SHOPS
(EXAMPLES OF)

Drum Kit
(near-perfect condition)

Tiny Baby
Clothes

– Why would someone give them to a thrift shop if they were wanted?

– They *are* wanted. They're wanted by the thrift shop. I'm talking about books that no one wants! I'm talking about books that have never been read! I'm talking about books that no one wants to read!

– OK. So there are some books that no one wants to read. What's the big deal?

Windup
Teeth Toy

Old Records

Old Family Portraits

Frog
Puppet
(some cosmetic
wear)

Telepathy Helmet
(needs rewiring)

– **Because without a reader a book is nothing! Do you know what happens to books that no one wants to read? Has anyone told you?**

You shake your head.

– **I didn't think so. Do you want to know? Because the truth is pretty shocking. Not too many people like to talk about it. But I'm here to give it to you straight, so here it is. If a book is unwanted, if it is considered *surplus to requirements*, they ship us to a warehouse in the middle of nowhere, and, just like that, we're murdered. That's right. *Murder*. Only they don't call it that. They have a fancy word for it: *pulped*.* They think using the same word as the gross bit of a smoothie can cover up what they're doing.**

– **Do I look like a smoothie?!**

---

*Which means they strip off your cover, shred you into a billion bits, and mash you into mush.

Fig. 39

MELONY OR MISDEMEANOR

You shake your head harder, more than a little scared. Though you *would* like a smoothie.

– Oh, people try and dress it up as "recycling." They claim that the paper in you—your very body!—can be used for something more useful. Like toilet paper.

– Let me ask you, would *you* like to be turned into toilet paper?

– I don't think so.

Fig. 40: TOILET PAPER
(AMOUNT USED IN AN AVERAGE LIFE SPAN)

– If people don't think you look interesting, they don't kill you and then use you to wipe their bum, do they?

– Not so far.

– So if you think I'm a little obsessed with whether people are or are not "bookist"—which *is* a thing—just remember that we're talking about *my life* here!

Your neck is getting tired. You take a shake break. Although you'd rather have a smoothie. Smoothies are the best.

– So *that* is why I hide up here.

– So that no one will wipe their bum with you?

– So that no one will notice me!

– Oh.

– And then you had to ruin it!

Then you hear a strange fluttering sound. The sound of paper crinkling and a kind of sniffing. What's that sound? Is it *crying*? Can a book cry?

You dash up the ladder for a closer listen.

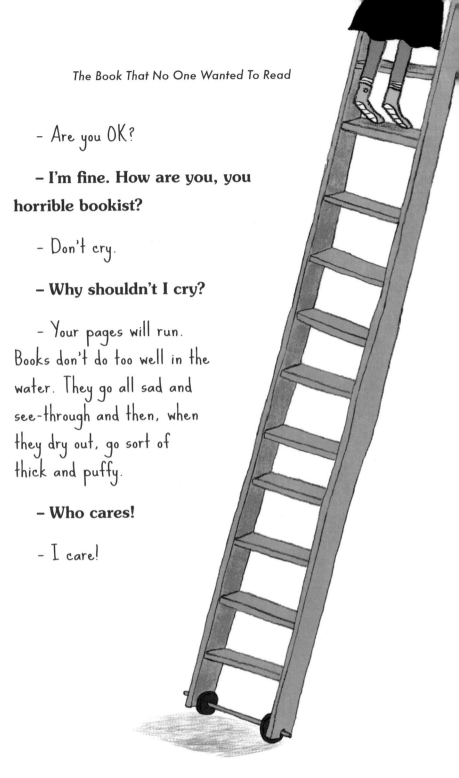

\- Are you OK?

– I'm fine. How are you, you horrible bookist?

\- Don't cry.

– Why shouldn't I cry?

\- Your pages will run. Books don't do too well in the water. They go all sad and see-through and then, when they dry out, go sort of thick and puffy.

– Who cares!

\- I care!

79

Fig. 41

BOOKS IN WATER

(A STUDY)

– Why do you care?

– Because I'd like to read you.

– You don't even know what I'm about!

– Well, I'd like to find out.

– What if you don't like me?

– I'm going to like you.

– How do you know?

– Because I already do.

And with that, you reach out, open the book, and look within.

CHAPTER SEVEN

IN WHICH YOU AND THE BOOK COME TO AN AGREEMENT OF SORTS

You start flicking through the pages. You flick and flick until you can flick no more (i.e., you flick through all the pages).

- You're completely empty!

– Empty? Well thanks a lot! Empty! You're not so deep yourself!

- No. I mean, there's nothing written on your pages.

– Is it because I've been crying?

Not that I've been crying. But do you think someone's tears, say the tears of another book, could have washed all the words away?

– No. Your pages are completely blank. If there had been ink here, there'd be smudges or marks. I'm always spilling stuff, so I know all about this. Yeah. People say spilling is bad, but sometimes it can help you find stuff out, like one time I spilled some really sticky—

You gasp.

Fig. 42

INK
BOTTLES
(VARIOUS)

Vermillion

MAYBE PINK

Magenta

ROSE

- That's it! The reason no one wants to read you is because you haven't been *written* yet! You have no contents.

– No need to be rude.

- I just meant that you're blank.

– Gosh, you sure know how to kick a book when it's down.

- I don't mean to upset you.

– So no one will *ever* read me. Hope, thou hast dissolved like a lozenge in lava, like a guff in a breeze.

- But this means you have potential! This means you could be anything!

– **An open book, as it were . . .**

- Exactly! So, what would you like to be?

– **I've never considered it. What *could* I be?**

- You could be a spy book, about a brilliant undercover agent named Bibi Agnes, the Brave Adventurer.

– **I'm not too keen on alliterative names. You know—when characters are called Anthony Anteater—I find it overly convenient.**

- All right, what would you call the special agent?

– **Well, he or she should have a name that no one would remark upon. Like Bob.**

Fig. 43

SPY MYSTERY
BOOK COVER

- Any surname?

– No. It would just be one name. Like Elvis. But instead of Elvis, the spy would be named Bob.

- So it would be a spy book about someone named Bob.

– Yes. It could be called *My Name Is Bob, and I'm a Spy.*

- But if Bob is a spy, why would he tell everyone?

– Maybe he's not very good at being a spy. Ooh! What if the book was called *My Name Is Bob, and I'm Not a Good Spy?*

- Hmmm . . . What about romance? You could be a romance book!

– Does that involve kissing?

- It might . . .

– Count me out of any canoodling!

Fig. 44
ROMANCE BOOK COVER

- Not even a super tiny kissy-kiss?

– Definitely not!

- OK. What about adventure?

– Did I mention I have allergies?

- No, but it makes sense now that you say it.

– Did I mention my fear of lows?

- Lows?

– Yes, lows. Many people are frightened of heights. Not me. I like heights. I've gotten used to being up here, safely out of reach. No danger of being knocked over or plucked out or dropped onto the floor. So I wouldn't want to be a book that was in any way about people who touched the ground.

- That could end up being tricky. Even pilots or astronauts have to come back to earth eventually.

90

Fig. 45

ADVENTURE BOOK COVER

– Oh, it's no use. I can't be a book *and* an author. Only a genius could do that!*

- You know, you don't have to *be* the story you tell? That writers aren't the same as their books? J.K. Rowling isn't actually a wizard.

Wand

Hat with star motif

Ability to break bounds of reality

Half-moon glasses

Cat colleague

Beard

Chair (not magic, but nice to sit in)

Cloak

Fig. 46: SOME PROPERTIES OF A (REAL) WIZARD

*Ahem . . . [blushes]

– **I was under the impression that you had to write what you know, and all I know is how to be a book that no one wants to read.**

– You're thinking of autobiography! A story can be about anything! You don't have to do the things in the story in order to write a story. You can write a story about a dragon without actually being a dragon. Otherwise there would be no stories about dragons!

– **I just presumed that books about dragons were written by dragons.**

– Well, they're not.

– **Seems strange.**

– How would a dragon hold a pen?

– **By going to dragon school?**

– People *imagined* dragons. Fearsome ones. And sparkly unicorns.

Fig. 47

DRAGON SCHOOL

– Well, whoop-de-doo for people.

You've got this book on the ropes. The poor thing doesn't stand a chance. You press home your advantage.

– I have an idea.

– Good for you.

– Do you want to hear it?

– How would I know? I don't know what it is yet.

This book needs you. In fact, you're what this book has been *waiting* for.

– I thought, perhaps, I could help to write you.

– Write me?

– Yes. With your permission of course. I wouldn't just . . .

– Despoil me?

– No. I would never do that. What does *despoil* mean?

– In this case I guess it would mean "scribble on."

– I'm too old for scribbling. We would sort of . . . talk it over first.

– What kind of thing would we write?

– Ooh, I don't know. We'd come up with something.

– And who would the reader be?

– Not sure yet. Us at first.

– And maybe if it's just for us, that's OK, too . . .

- Exactly.

– **A story we tell ourselves.**

- The best kind.

– **A story that maybe . . . someday . . .**
would be big enough to fill a whole book.

Fig. 48
SCRIBBLES
(A STUDY)

- If we spaced it out.

– And pictures help.

- They do.

Fig. 49: HELPFUL PICTURE

Fig. 50: UNHELPFUL PICTURE

Fig. 51: A PICTURE THAT'S NO HELP AT ALL

You and the book fall silent at the enormity of it all. But not for too long.

– Imagine if I were a Book That People Wanted To Read. It's unthinkable.

– I think it's thinkable.

– Really?

– I'm already thinking it.

– I wonder what we should call me?

– Let's not worry about that yet.

– You're right. The title's always the last thing.

And with that, you climb down the ladder, holding your new friend tight, in much the same way I hope you are holding me now.

THE END

EPILOGUE

IN WHICH I ASK BOTH "WHAT WAS THE POINT OF ALL THAT?" AND FURTHERMORE, "WHAT IS THE POINT OF POINTS?"

Sometimes you know the point of a story as soon as it starts.

"Not so long ago, there was a hyena who took things a little too seriously . . ."

We know (don't we) the type of turns this tale will take. The serious hyena will wind up doing something where it really *helps* if you're serious, quite boring, and rarely ever laugh. Like being a parent. Well maybe not all parents. But definitely the ones who say "at the end of the day" even when they're being boring in the morning.

Parents *love* points.

And parents love stories that make a point. They sometimes act as if the story was *in the way of the point.* Before they've even gotten to the end of the story, they'll ask, "What *point* do you think the author is trying to make?" They call it comprehension. I call it distraction.

What (I'd like to ask *them*) is the *point* of all these points?*

Take the story of "The Scorpion and the Frog."

A scorpion and a frog are by a river and the scorpion says, "Look here, Hoppy, how's about giving me a lift across? I've left my water wings at a friend's house."

So the frog says, "One, a little less of the Hoppy

---

*This is also my question to the porcupine.

and two, no offense, but aren't scorpions famous for stinging people left, right, and (perhaps most painfully) center? Which is bad enough under normal circumstances, but even worse when carrying cargo across yonder river."

So the scorpion says, "Look, Croaky, why would I sting you whilst crossing yonder river? If I sting you, you'll sink into the drink and take me down for the dive."

So the frog says, "One, a little less of the Croaky but, two, I now feel completely reassured."

So the scorpion clambers aboard and the frog gets going with his best breaststroke.

Halfway across, the scorpion stings the frog.

As they both begin to sink, the frog says (perhaps after some stronger words of reproach), "Why did you *do* that?"

To which the scorpion replies, "It's my nature."

The Scorpion
A Savage Saga

and the Frog: of Betrayal

The End

What (I ask you) is the "point" of this story?

We get it: scorpions sting and it's hard to swim when you're dead, so maybe don't let scorpions set up shop in your trunks.

Did we really need a whole fable about it?

I can't exactly explain the point of The Book That No One Wanted To Read. I think (if pressed) the *real* point was to spend some time with you. You see, I feel we've always understood each other, you and I. Almost telepathically. And I like the idea of you imagining what might be written on The Book's blank pages. You see, blank pages might look like a big pile of nothing, but they're actually a doorway to anything you might wish to dream. A gleaming white doorway that (OK sure) looks a bit like paper.

You can't open this magical doorway with a mere key. Because (as I think is clear by now) we're actually talking about paper.

Fig. 52

NOTHING

(IN PILES)

You need imagination, some time, and a tiny bit of courage.

Oh, and a pen.*

So what are you waiting for?

And if you *do* write a book that makes a point, make a point of making it fun.

Otherwise there's no point at all.

Fig. 53: PEN
(SLIDING DOWN AN INVISIBLE HILL)

*Pen not provided.

RICHARD AYOADE

Richard Ayoade wrote this book. He has written others, but they were not this one. Which is probably for the best. You can only write the same book for so long before someone finds out. These days, if he sits down, it's not too long before he's asleep.

TOR FREEMAN

Tor Freeman illustrated this book. She has illustrated lots of other books, and also she draws and writes comics. She likes drawing animals in clothes, sewing, and running. These days, if she sits down, it's not too long before she's asleep.